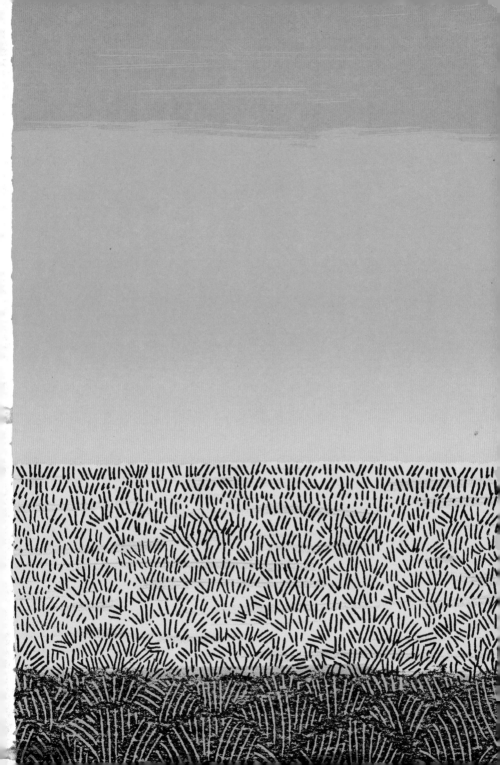

Also by Andi Watson

Glister
Princess Decomposia and Count Spatula

Kerry

and the Knight of the Forest

Cover art, text, and interior illustrations copyright © 2020 by Andi Watson

All rights reserved. Published in the United States by RH Graphic, an imprint of Random House Children's Books, a division of Penguin Random House LLC, New York.

RH Graphic with the book design is a trademark of Penguin Random House LLC.

Visit us on the Web! RHKidsGraphic.com • @RHKidsGraphic

Educators and librarians, for a variety of teaching tools, visit us at RHTeachersLibrarians.com

Library of Congress Cataloging-in-Publication Data
Names: Watson, Andi, author.
Title: Kerry and the knight of the forest / Andi Watson.
Description: First edition. | New York : RH Graphic, [2020] | Audience: Ages 8–12 | Audience: Grades 4–6 | Summary: "Kerry gets lost on his way home and has to navigate through a fantastical forest to find his way out, only most of the creatures in the forest are not there to help him"—Provided by publisher.
Identifiers: LCCN 2019025827 | ISBN 978-1-9848-9330-7 (library binding) | ISBN 978-0-593-12523-6 (hardcover) | ISBN 978-1-9848-9329-1 (paperback) | ISBN 978-1-9848-9331-4 (ebook)
Subjects: LCSH: Graphic novels. | CYAC: Graphic novels. | Lost children—Fiction. | Forests and forestry—Fiction. | Fantasy.
Classification: LCC PZ7.7.W375 Ke 2020 | DDC 741.5/973—dc23

Designed by Patrick Crotty

MANUFACTURED IN CHINA
10 9 8 7 6 5 4 3 2 1
First Edition

RH GRAPHIC

A comic on every bookshelf.

Huf

HuFF
PuFF.

HuFF
PuFF.

Meadowsweet, do you know it?

It's my village.

Where my family lives.

My name's Kerry.

Who are you?

I need to find the quickest way there.

Come on, they're about to start the game.

21

Though this is the shorter route.

You might be home before sunset.

Where are you?

I can't see you.

Carrrk!

Wah!

Nnngth.

Not ... going to ... let go.

Carrrk.

What do you think you are doing?

Me? Nothing. Only **SWAPPING SECRETS** with my **SNAIL FRIEND.**

Hush, hush, please.

I'm not going anywhere until you show me the way to get home.

Please remove your behind from my house and I will tell you.

Thank you. See how easy it is when we agree to help each other?

Look for the Old Knight of the Road.

Look where?

Follow Mocktree Dell by Ravensmead Hollow through Bicton Trough behind Odding's Copse.

Slow down. Raven's Trough behind Dell Hollow?

Fry me in butter. I will say no more.

Thanks a lot for your help.

I'll find the knight myself.

How hard can it be? It's not as though a knight will blend into the background.

Mocktree Dell.

Mocktree Dell.

What does a dell look like, anyway?

And how do you tell a dell from a hollow?

A bite to eat and back to it.

ZzZzZzz.

Hello?

Zzz...Snorrr...zzz.

Zzzzzz.

WHO? Oh...err...me.

WHO is me?

Kerry.

Kerry? Who is this Kerry?

Kerry is lost. No, what I mean is, I'm lost.

And that's reason enough to wake a stranger from their slumber?

I'm looking for someone.

Hurling missiles is how you go about it?

I didn't know what else to do.

I'm sorry, should I have knocked?

KNOCKED? I'm not a farm door. You might have begun by saying hello.

I did say hello. You didn't hear me. You were snoring.

Was I?

C...cast what aside?

The thornberry fruit you are about to poison yourself with.

It's poisonous?

Urgh.

As are all the fruits of the forest. And the springs, streams, and brooks. The foxhead nettles, banebind, violet rose, and ash crowns.

A child who eats thornberries and listens to talking snails. It is no surprise that the forest swallowed you whole.

It wasn't until I lost sight of her that I knew I'd been tricked.

Who is her?

The girl. She told me this way would get me home quickest.

And you believed her?

You don't know where he is?

It so happens I do.

You do?

Can you show me the way?

He wouldn't thank me to send every stranger to his abode. Not all of those who blunder their way into the forest are deserving.

I might not be deserving, but my family is.

They are sick with the fever. I'm on my way back from the Wise Woman with their medicine, and the longer I delay my return, the more I fear it will be too late.

The knight isn't without a heart; he knows pluck when he sees it.

The sun could stretch its fingers to the forest floor in those days.

All the creatures of the forest, the squirrels, deer, and hedgepigs would cross my paths.

The butterflies would alight on me before dusk, when the bats would take their turn in the air.

And then there were the children, of course.

They would climb their favorite trees and play their games.

I would hear their laughter and cries echoing between the boughs throughout the seasons.

I'd carry the little ones on my back, take them home if they played out late.

They'd fall asleep there as I returned them *safely home...*

Raised from hardy stock, aren't we, son?

Yes.

I've had a raging thirst all day.

Hmm, it smells...

of nothing.

Stop sniffing it, son, and eat up.

Sit yourself down, son.

No reflection.

If I'm not here...

I followed your trail of trampled undergrowth and broken branches.

I had hoped to keep your presence in the forest a secret, but my plans are undone.

Now every creep, sneak, and wretch knows you are here.

They do?

Come.

All the shadows of the forest are allied against you. We must make haste if you aren't to be captured.

The birds ceased their song, and the local people whispered stories from the safety of their cottages.

Eventually the very trees themselves were silenced.

Folk warned their children away from the forest.

There were those who thought themselves brave who entered the woods and never returned.

The wisps, snags, snitches, and banes crawled into the places left by the badger, deer, and hedgepigs.

Now you see the forest not as it was, teeming with life, but as it has become, corrupted and malicious.

What made it this way?

It's the work of a malevolent spirit who has influence over everything within the forest.

All the beasts that lurk in the shade of the trees report to it. The wisp was its vassal, and now that the Spirit knows you are here, it will do everything to ensure you never leave.

What about the girl— she does the Spirit's bidding?

It will use any trick to lure the unwary.

I tell you I will never conspire with this Spirit.

Do not be so quick to judge.

101

Phew.

Don't worry, I had a soft landing.

I'll find my own way back.

I can't get free of the little creeps.

ᒥᑎᑫᖾ

Get...

off.

I have never known Seedlings to act in this way. I fear the Spirit is directing all its malice at you.

Perhaps so.

Henceforth we must be more wary.

Hold on, there's some —

Not this one. See, it's friendly.

You have no friends in the forest.

I have you.

I hear grumbling, but it's not coming from any wolves.

Very well. If you insist on putting every possible obstacle in the way of your freedom.

Don't worry, you'll be safe with us.

||/|\|

Didn't you want to fight back?

Certainly I fought.

I am a guide, not a warrior.

I have no weapons nor desire to harm any living thing, even the spiteful and wicked.

Perhaps that is why my presence is tolerated.

You didn't help the children who were taken?

I believed if I did not intefere, then I would not provoke the Spirit to greater evil.

In the end I made myself scarce.

You didn't miss helping travelers?

I decided I could not be of assistance.

It sounds awfully lonely to me.

When I'm alone, I can tell myself it's because I choose to be, but really it's because my mother and father are out in the fields.

I know I'm not really alone because they'll soon burst through the door, kick the dirt off their boots, and we'll sit together and eat.

Fee-Fi-Fo-Fum.

Then we'll sing or tell stories of the trip to market or the funny thing one of the cows did...

...I don't know what I'll do if I never see them again.

If there's no one waiting for me at home.

One morning my father couldn't raise himself from bed. He begged us to leave, but my mother nursed him until she caught the fever too.

Their faces burned hot as coals, and their teeth chattered like there was a winter frost. I fetched water and food, but they couldn't eat or drink.

I did the best I could.

I was scared. Scared to leave them alone and scared to travel to Lydgate to find the wise woman.

I promised them I'd return with the medicine.

134

You're back to haunt me?

Come along, Kerry.

137

When it's time, I want you to flee.

Is it time yet?

They have
long legs.

It looks like they've gone.

Thank you for saving me back there.

!/\/!

We'll stay here and wait for the Waystone to find us.

Wait!

Where's my bag?

My bag!

I'll have to go back for it.

You stay here.

\||||

It's too dangerous.

\||||

No. Stay!

I'm sorry but you need to stay here where it's safe.

I'll come back for you.

)(|)(|

I will.

I promise.

Didn't I tell you to run?

Waystone.

I got away, but those things have stolen my bag.

They are the Gorse folk. As you saw, they are adept at springing traps.

We have to follow before they get too far away.

That is precisely what the Spirit wants you to do, deliver yourself up to it and spare it the effort.

I don't care what the Spirit expects, I'm going.

Then all our struggles have been for naught.

Without the medicine, I've failed.

I can't go home empty-handed.

How can you know your mother and father are not recovered from their malady and worry every moment at your absence?

I know that without the medicine they'll die, and if they die, then I'll stay in this rotten forest with the rotten Spirit because I'll have nothing to go back for.

Sniff.

As a rule I do not make promises. They are as easily spun as a lie.

However, I tell you this: I promise you will have your medicine.

You promise?

I have a way of guiding those who have gone astray.

I can just as well bend my skill toward finding a lost bag.

Thank you.

Thank you.

Thank you.

Very well.

You managed to get away?

The Gorse are dogged but not the most quick-witted of foes.

How did they know we were coming?

Something or someone must have alerted them.

Those forest children?

It is possible they delayed us long enough for the ambush to be set.

Well, it didn't work this time.

The spirit is cunning; it will not give up so easily.

Where do we go from here?

There is a little-known route.

I had hoped never to take this path, but if we are to avoid an ambush at every turn, we must steer our way through an area of the forest where even the Spirit's minions dare not venture.

Why not?

I have heard talk, but it is only talk.

It's not safe, then?

Safety is far behind us and we are far from it. My concern is that it is the route the Spirit wishes us to take.

I have to go back for the seedling.

It may have been the seedling who betrayed us.

It wouldn't. Would it? Anyway, I promised I'd go back for it.

I can't leave it there all on its own, waiting for me.

That would be awful.

Come, little one.

The swamp is no place for a child.

What sort of guardian puts their ward in harm's way?

I only wish to bring you home safely.

You're what's making it sick.

That is the gratitude you receive for doing the creature a kindness.

I don't mind. At least I've helped someone in this rotten place.

We're sinking!

Thank you for the ride.

Bye.

Where do we go now?

Waystone?

It is but a short distance to your destination.

No matter what it is, I'll help you. Nothing will get the better of us.

Be on your way.

You made a promise, remember?

I did.

That you would find the medicine. You promised that.

I did.

Then you'll break your word?

If you insist on holding me to an idle promise, then I cannot go back on it.

Then I insist.

You will regret your decision.

Then you're coming with me?

You will not thank me.

What is it?

How artless the little ones are.

The...the Spirit?

Come now, old friend.

What have you to say?

This is the end of our journey together, Kerry.

Old Friend?

The Waystone and I have an agreement.

I have a family of my own.

Forget them.

I will be both a mother and father to you now.

And look, here are your brothers and sisters.

Don't be shy, there's a good girl.

I did not want to do what I did.

I will stay with you, here in the forest, if you set the children free.

Why, you speak as though I keep them in chains.

You call it a family, but families don't stay together out of fear.

They do so out of choice.

Out of love.

Forgive me.

I only speak out of love.

If you set them free, I promise I will stay with you.

Waystone!

NO!

Ah!

Off you go, then.

And do take care in the forest.

Quickly, before it changes its mind.

You never told me your name.

I'm called Bea.

I will tell your family of your courage.

Alas, it is bittersweet when the fledglings leave the nest.

Do not envy them, little one. Their fates are certain.

See.

Their teeth will come loose, their faces will fall, and their bones will crumble.

Sickness and disease will claim them all.

I am everything to you now.

I'm sorry about your family.

They would have made me regret my actions. Betraying a child on their behalf would only have brought shame on us all.

I don't blame you. You've been alone a long time.

LOOK!

Already they are returning.

IF you hurry, you will catch the other children.

Oh, wait.

Come on out.

There you are.

Waystone?

Waystone!

I did remember the way.

Kerry!

What brings you back to the Forest?

THE END

Kerry and the Knight of the Forest was drawn and lettered with Uni Pin pens, a blunt compass tip, and chinagraph pencils on 200g A5 sheets of fine grain paper. It was colored using Photoshop CS6 and a Wacom Bamboo tablet.

7	SPEED
9	EMPATHY
8	STEALTH
10	MOXIE
7	SMARTS
3	STRENGTH

SKILLS

Aim/throw

Farming

Understands animals

INFORMATION

Kerry leaves home for the first time to fetch medicine for his sick parents when he gets lost in the woods.

KERRY

6	SPEED
8	EMPATHY
5	STEALTH
8	MOXIE
8	SMARTS
9	STRENGTH

SKILLS

Pathfinding

Tracking

Forest wisdom

INFORMATION

A living rock with the ability to find a way through the impenetrable Forest of Shadows.

WAYSTONE

1	SPEED
2	EMPATHY
4	STEALTH
3	MOXIE
6	SMARTS
2	STRENGTH

SKILLS

Hide inside its shell

Forest wisdom

INFORMATION

A nervous forest denizen and reluctant helper to kerry.

SNAIL

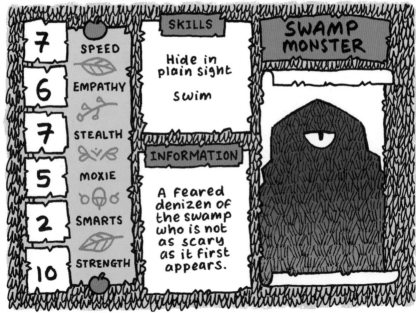

7	SPEED
6	EMPATHY
7	STEALTH
5	MOXIE
2	SMARTS
10	STRENGTH

SKILLS

Hide in plain sight

Swim

INFORMATION

A feared denizen of the swamp who is not as scary as it first appears.

SWAMP MONSTER

6	SPEED
7	EMPATHY
4	STEALTH
7	MOXIE
8	SMARTS
6	STRENGTH

SKILLS

Farming

Animal husbandry

Parenting

INFORMATION

When they are both struck down by a fever, Kerry has to find a cure and return home in time.

KERRY'S MUM & DAD

8	SPEED
3	EMPATHY
6	STEALTH
5	MOXIE
4	SMARTS
3	STRENGTH

SKILLS

Fly

Dive-bomb

INFORMATION

The bird sits high up in the trees and spies for the Spirit. Likes to eat snails.

BLACKBIRD

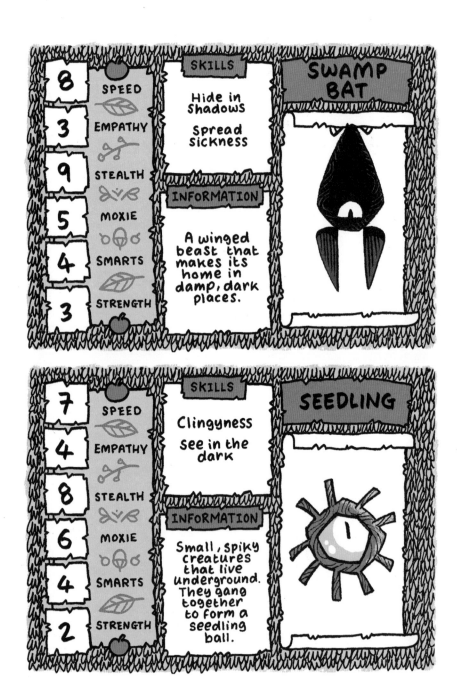

SWAMP BAT

8	SPEED
3	EMPATHY
9	STEALTH
5	MOXIE
4	SMARTS
3	STRENGTH

SKILLS

Hide in Shadows

Spread Sickness

INFORMATION

A winged beast that makes its home in damp, dark places.

SEEDLING

7	SPEED
4	EMPATHY
8	STEALTH
6	MOXIE
4	SMARTS
2	STRENGTH

SKILLS

Clingyness

See in the dark

INFORMATION

Small, spiky creatures that live underground. They gang together to form a seedling ball.

6	SPEED
7	EMPATHY
8	STEALTH
7	MOXIE
5	SMARTS
1	STRENGTH

SKILLS

Clingyness

See in the dark

INFORMATION

Stowing away in kerry's bag, it joins the search for a way out of the forest.

LITTLE SEEDLING

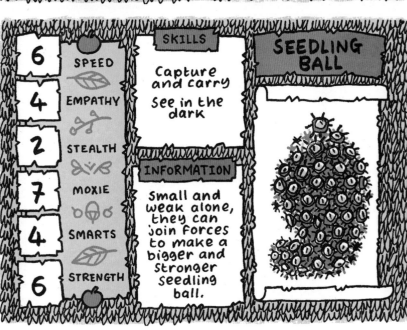

6	SPEED
4	EMPATHY
2	STEALTH
7	MOXIE
4	SMARTS
6	STRENGTH

SKILLS

Capture and carry

See in the dark

INFORMATION

Small and weak alone, they can join forces to make a bigger and stronger seedling ball.

SEEDLING BALL

8	SPEED
2	EMPATHY
6	STEALTH
4	MOXIE
5	SMARTS
1	STRENGTH

SKILLS

Hypnotize

Create illusions

INFORMATION

These beautiful balls of light lure unwary travelers deeper into the forest until captured by the Spirit.

WILL-O-WISP

0

6	SPEED
3	EMPATHY
9	STEALTH
5	MOXIE
3	SMARTS
7	STRENGTH

SKILLS

Hide in plain sight

Tracking

INFORMATION

Disguising themselves as bushes, the Gorse Folk lie in wait to attack those who have lost their way.

GORSE FOLK

SPIRIT OF THE FOREST

9	SPEED
4	EMPATHY
9	STEALTH
5	MOXIE
10	SMARTS
2	STRENGTH

SKILLS

Hypnotize

Create illusions

Lightning Strike

INFORMATION

A malicious spirit which has corrupted the forest and rules over all of the creatures that live within it.

FOREST CHILDREN

6	SPEED
7	EMPATHY
8	STEALTH
3	MOXIE
6	SMARTS
2	STRENGTH

SKILLS

Mislead

Hide in plain sight

INFORMATION

Children lured into the forest by the spirit and held there at the whim of their captor.

CREATE YOUR OWN CHARACTER

? SPEED	**SKILLS**
? EMPATHY	Put skills or abilities here
? STEALTH	**INFORMATION**
? MOXIE	Some background on your character here
? SMARTS	
? STRENGTH	

Name here

Draw a picture of your character here

Trace onto a separate sheet ↓

- Assign your character a number between one and ten for each characteristic.

- Are they an animal, a creature or a person? Are they you?

- Give at least one characteristic a low number. If they are very strong, then they might have low stealth or speed.

- Note down their skills and a little bit about them in the information box.

- Draw a picture of your character.

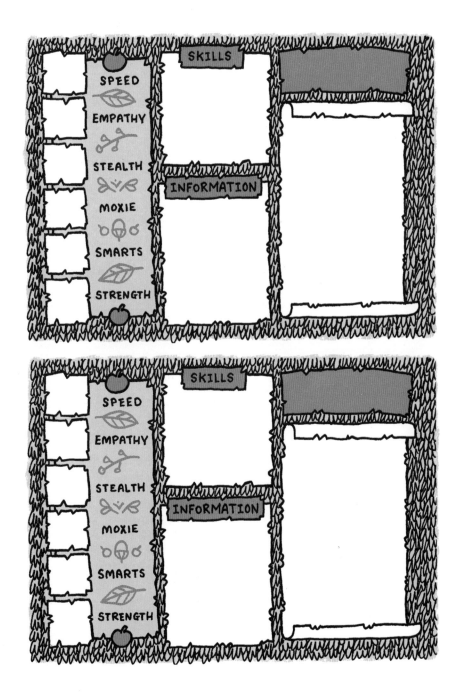

SKILLS

SPEED

EMPATHY

STEALTH

MOXIE

SMARTS

STRENGTH

INFORMATION

SKILLS

SPEED

EMPATHY

STEALTH

MOXIE

SMARTS

STRENGTH

INFORMATION

These are pages from an early attempt at this story a number of years ago. I'd picked it up and put it aside several times, including thumbnailing out an entire graphic novel before abandoning it.

The fairy tale idea of the child lost in the woods wouldn't go away, though. Eventually I took it up again with the idea of the Waystone and it finally came together. Sometimes a story has to sit and stew a long time before it's ready.

One thing that remained consistent throughout the development of the book was a way of drawing that would incorporate texture and pattern.

Kerry began as a very simple design, more of a symbol, like a pawn on a chessboard, than a person. I needed to add detail and bring him to life.

This is my first book to be in full color, and so I experimented with different ways to use it and what kind of color palette I was going to employ. Here I used an inkpad and sponge to get the murky effect.

I studied graphic design and illustration at college and love the process of designing book covers. I tend to do lots of little thumbnail sketches to work out the best combinations of words and image. I find a cover that works well as a tiny sketch will often make an eye-catching cover design that will stand out on the bookshelves. Patrick (the designer) and I tried lots of different ideas before settling on the right one.

These are some of the development sketches I drew up in order to help visualize what the other characters and settings in the story would look like. I worked on giving Kerry more individuality and figured out how to bring a rock personality. They were stepping-stones on the way to the final designs. A finished book is only the visible tip of a mountain of sketches, scripts, and wrong turns.

Thank you to Gina, Whitney, Patrick, and the whole team at RHG for helping make this book happen.

Andi Watson was born and raised in a small town in the north of England, where he loved to draw and read books. As a kid, he read the Star Wars and Beano comic books. As a teenager, he read fantasy trilogies and obsessed over Dungeons & Dragons. He rediscovered comics while at art school, amazed by series like Akira and Love and Rockets. At the very end of his degree, he decided to make his own comic, as this would be his only opportunity before taking up a career in illustration. It didn't quite work out that way, as many years later he is still telling stories with words and pictures, this being his thirtieth book. He has created comics for grown-ups and children and those somewhere in between. These include stand-alone graphic novels for adults such as *Breakfast After Noon* and *Slow News Day*, series for teenagers like Skeleton Key, and series for children like Glister and Gum Girl. He's occasionally been nominated for awards and has had books translated into French, Spanish, German, and Italian. He still enjoys reading and drawing. He lives in Worcester, England, with his wife and daughter, where he drinks tea and is trying to learn French (again).

@andicomics
andiwatson.info

RH GRAPHIC

· THE SUMMER 2020 LIST ·

CRABAPPLE TROUBLE
By Kaeti Vandorn

· · · · · · · · ·

Life isn't easy when you're an apple.

Callaway and Thistle must figure out how to work together—with delicious and magical results.

Young Chapter Book

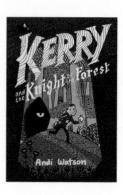

KERRY AND THE KNIGHT OF THE FOREST
By Andi Watson

· · · · · · · · · · ·

Kerry needs to get home!

To get back to his parents, Kerry gets lost in a shortcut. He will have to make tough choices and figure out who to trust—or remain lost in the forest . . . forever.

Middle Grade

STEPPING STONES
By Lucy Knisley

· · · · · · · · ·

Jen did not want to leave the city.

She did not want to move to a farm.

And Jen definitely did not want to get two new "sisters."

Middle Grade

SUNCATCHER
By Jose Pimienta

· · · · · · · · ·

Beatriz loves music—more than her school, more than her friends—and she won't let anything stop her from achieving her dreams.

Even if it means losing everything else.

Young Adult

FIND US ONLINE AT @RHKIDSGRAPHIC AND RHKIDSGRAPHIC.COM